True Heart

MARISSA MOSS

Illustrated by C. F. Payne

Silver Whistle

Harcourt Brace & Company

San Diego   New York   London

Requests for permission to make copies of any part of the work
should be mailed to: Permissions Department, Harcourt Brace & Company,
6277 Sea Harbor Drive, Orlando, Florida 32887-6777.

Library of Congress Cataloging-in-Publication Data
Moss, Marissa.
True Heart/Marissa Moss; illustrated by C. F. Payne.
p. cm.
"Silver Whistle."
Summary: At the turn of the century, a young woman who works on the railroad
accomplishes her yearning ambition to become an engineer when a
male engineer is injured and can't drive his train.
ISBN 0-15-201344-X
[1. Locomotive engineers—Fiction. 2. Sex role—Fiction. 3. West (U.S.)—Fiction.]
I. Payne, C. F., ill. II. Title.
PZ7.M8535Tr 1999
[Fic]—dc20   95-50866

First edition
A C E F D B
Printed in Hong Kong

The illustrations in this book were done in mixed media.
The display type was hand lettered by Tom Seibert.
The text type was set in Goudy Village.
Color separations by Bright Arts Ltd., Hong Kong
Printed by South China Printing Company, Ltd., Hong Kong
This book was printed on totally chlorine-free Nymolla Matte Art paper.
Production supervision by Stanley Redfern and Ginger Boyer
Designed by Lisa Peters

To Helen, making a journey of her own
—M. M.

To my parents, Pete and Martha Payne,
for their gift to me of life—and to my wife, Paula,
and kids, Trevor and Evan, for their gift of love
for the present and future
—C. F. P.

THIS IS MY favorite photograph, the one of me and my work crew loading pipe into a freight train. It's not that I loved loading trains more than driving them. Oh no, I'm mighty glad to be an engineer, and I worked hard to get to be one, too. But I like to remember those days when becoming an engineer was a faraway wish, like one you'd make on a star on a clear summer's night.

It's good to remember wanting something so much you can't think of anything else. It makes me grin, because my wish came true. It took a while, but it did. I've been working on the railroad since I was sixteen. That was in 1893, the year my mother and father died from the typhus, and I was left with eight brothers and sisters to raise. I've always been strong and hard work doesn't scare me, but I needed to earn good money to provide for my family. At first I got a job doing washing, but I saw that railroad work paid much better. That's when I decided to load freight for the Union Pacific.

At first the railroad didn't want to hire me, but they saw I was good and they needed my muscles. So there I was, loading pipe and machinery, bolts of cloth, and dry goods. It wasn't long before others, hearing of the good pay, came to work with me. Soon there were ten of us loading freight together: me, Blackie, Snubs, Georgie, Big Dee, Cookie, G. G, Freddy, Woody, and Bear.

I loved being part of the railroad. When my parents came out to Cheyenne from Minnesota, there wasn't any way to cross this country except by wagon or walking. Now there are trains joining together the two ends of this great nation, and everyone, everything, goes by train.

And the trains are so beautiful, painted all pretty — gussied up
with curtains and lace in the dining cars and snoozers. Real elegant.
I loved to be near them, to hear their clatter and roar, and to imagine
the cities they came from, the frontiers they were going to.

But I wanted to do more than imagine. I wanted to be an engineer and ride those trains to big cities with names like Wichita and St. Louis, and to roar into small towns with names like Silver Ridge and Devil's Bowl. Just hearing those names set my mind to spinning, imagining great big buildings and bright red cliffs.

Meanwhile, I sat in the cab whenever I could and closely watched the engineers work. And questions—I asked lots and lots of questions. Mr. Morgan called me a fly buzzing in his ear, but sometimes he would let me back up the engine and couple it to cars on the side tracks. Ole Pete was the best. He sometimes let me drive all the way to the next station. Then I'd hitch a ride back.

Snubs and Georgie teased me about it all the time.

"Hey, Engineer Bee!" they called as we loaded steel tools bound for California. "When are we gonna see you in the driver's seat for real? You tag after Ole Pete, begging for a turn, but here you are, still grunting with us." Snubs made pig noises, which wasn't hard with that snub nose.

"Don't worry about me," I replied. "I'll be an engineer someday, but while I'm waiting, I may as well grunt with you." I made my own pig snorts.

"Can you kindly stop them noises?" Blackie wailed. "You're making me hungry for a nice juicy pork chop. You'll be hearing my belly growl next. Won't that be a chorus!"

I laughed, but I knew I wouldn't be grunting forever. I waited and kept my eyes open.

I got my chance sooner than I thought. Here's what happened:

Train robberies weren't too uncommon in those days. Bandits would block the track, and when the train stopped, they'd board it and grab what they could — gold heading for banks back East or whatever riches the passengers carried.

That's what almost happened to the *True Heart* running from San Francisco to Chicago. This time the robbers shot at Ole Pete as he slowed down at a crossing. Pete sped up that train and got away, roaring into the next station, ours, in Cheyenne. He was hurt, and he stumbled out of the cab, clutching his arm. The coal feeder was wounded, too. That left the whole engine room empty.

Mr. Philips, the station manager, said he'd have to hold up the train till a new crew could be rustled up. I didn't waste any time. I knew this was my chance.

"Mr. Philips," I said, "I can drive that train, and Blackie and G. G. here can shovel the coal." G. G. looked at me like I was crazy, but Blackie grinned and gave me a big thumbs-up sign. Snubs and Georgie, they near dropped their jaws down to their knees, they were so surprised.

"No more grunting!" Cookie gave a big pig snort.

But Mr. Philips shook his head. "You know you can't do that. You're not an engineer."

"I've driven trains before," I said, "hitching them up to cars in the yard, taking them even as far as the next station."

Ole Pete nodded. "Bee's been in my cab many a time, asking questions, even taking over for short bits. I don't know more myself."

"That's different from flat-out driving," Mr. Philips said. "The answer is no."

The passengers began to yell, angry about being stopped over.

"Let 'er drive!" they called. "Come on! We don't want to sit here forever."

A big banker man took Mr. Philips aside, and his face was so red and angry and full of his own importance, I thought his hat would bust off and explode. I could see Mr. Philips arguing with him, then listening, then finally nodding his head. He turned toward me.

"All right, Bee," he growled. "You're an engineer today."

I nodded. "You won't be sorry, sir. I can do it!" I felt like laughing and singing all at once.

Blackie and G. G. hugged each other. Big Dee, Georgie, Snubs, Freddy, Cookie, Woody, and Bear all had grins so wide you could fit the entire night sky in them. Ole Pete winked at me. Tobacco Joe, who loaded freight, too, had big bug eyes. He couldn't believe what he saw—me, in Pete's engineer cap, climbing into the cab.

"Let's go," I called. "We've got a train to drive." Blackie and G. G. hopped in. The passengers and the conductor clambered back on. "And you," I called to Snubs and Georgie, "you owe me a nice juicy pork chop when we get back!"

"We'll be ready," they called. They all waved and blew kisses.

Blackie and G. G. started in on the coal. That fire was hot! Steam puffed out above us. I tugged on the whistle.

How I love that long, low sound, like the wind blowing down your back. *Whooooooo. Whooooooo.*

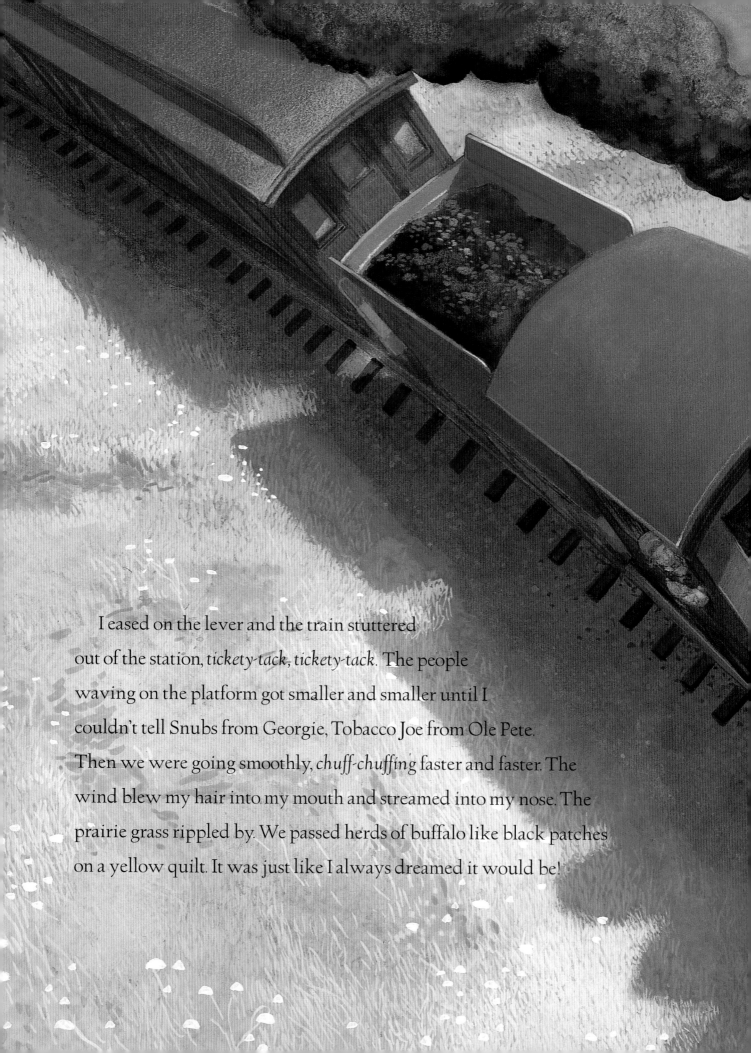

I eased on the lever and the train stuttered
out of the station, *tickety-tack, tickety-tack*. The people
waving on the platform got smaller and smaller until I
couldn't tell Snubs from Georgie, Tobacco Joe from Ole Pete.
Then we were going smoothly, *chuff-chuffing* faster and faster. The
wind blew my hair into my mouth and streamed into my nose. The
prairie grass rippled by. We passed herds of buffalo like black patches
on a yellow quilt. It was just like I always dreamed it would be!

Since then I've driven the *Golden State Limited,* the *Platte Valley Eagle,* the *Coyote Special,* and the *Roaring Wolf* with my crew, G. G. and Blackie. But my favorite is still the *True Heart.* Whenever we stop in Cheyenne, Snubs and Georgie greet me with a pork chop dinner. We eat and swap stories. My little brother Virgil is loading freight with them now. But he wants to be an engineer, like me. He always asks for, and I always tell him, like I just told you, the story of my first time, that first ride. I felt so free and strong, galloping across whole states in my iron horse, blowing my whistle for all the sky to hear.

Whoooooooooooo.

AUTHOR'S NOTE

THIS STORY WAS INSPIRED by an old photograph I saw at the California State Railroad Museum in Sacramento. It showed ten women in overalls posing in front of a freight car. There was no mistaking that they were a work crew. Intrigued, I met with Shirley Burman, a photographer who had curated the show *Women and the American Railroad*, from which the picture had come. I asked her who these women were — did many women work on the railroad? What did they do?

Ms. Burman generously offered all she knew. The women in the photo loaded freight for the Union Pacific in Cheyenne. In the Wyoming State Museum archive in Cheyenne, there are a few other photos of them carrying steel pipes. But no written records refer to them. As throughout much of history, women were a vital but invisible presence. There are records of a woman engineer working on the B & O, but she came after these Cheyenne women, who worked at the turn of the century.

To discover who these women might be, I read women's journals and letters from the period, especially those of western homesteaders who crossed the country in covered wagons.

There's no record of Bee, except for her proud, grinning face in the photos. I made up the name and the story, conjuring her personality out of the many women I met through their writings. But there's truth in fiction, and there's truth in the many stories of people like Bee — whose names we'll never know but can only imagine — people who had the determination to live out their dreams.